KIDS' SPORTS STORIES

AIM HIGH

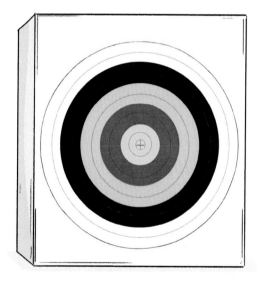

by Shawn Pryor

illustrated by Diego Funck

PICTURE WINDOW BOOKS
a capstone imprint

Kids' Sports Stories is published by Picture Window Books, an imprint of Capstone.
1710 Roe Crest Drive, North Mankato, Minnesota 56003
www.capstonepub.com

Library of Congress Cataloging-in-Publication Data is available on the Library of Congress website.
ISBN 978-1-5158-7095-1 (library binding)
ISBN 978-1-5158-7284-9 (paperback)
ISBN 978-1-5158-7130-9 (eBook PDF)

Summary: Friends Kerry and Zack can't get enough of their favorite superhero, a bow-and-arrow-toting character named Brave Bowie. Her magic arrows always save the day. But when the friends sign up for archery lessons, they soon learn that practice and hard work make real-life archers great in the sport, not cartoon tricks.

Designer: Ted Williams

33614082323642

Printed in the United States   4317

TABLE OF CONTENTS

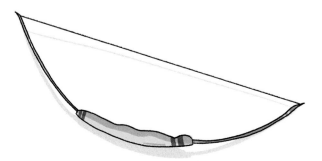

Glossary

 **archery**—the sport of shooting at targets using a bow and arrow

 **arrow**—a long, thin pointed stick that is shot with a bow

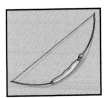 **bow**—a device for shooting arrows

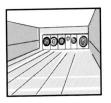 **range**—a place where archers meet and practice archery

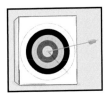 **target**—a marked object at which archers aim and shoot arrows

Chapter 1

BECOMING A SUPERHERO

Kerry and Zack were having a great afternoon. The two friends were watching their favorite TV show. It was about a superhero named Brave Bowie. She used her bow and arrows to fight evil.

"Brave Bowie is the best!" Kerry said.

"She can beat any bad guy!" Zack said.

In today's show, Brave Bowie tried to stop an evil doctor. But the doctor kept getting away. Finally, Brave Bowie grabbed one of her special arrows. She pulled back her bowstring. She aimed at the doctor's feet and shot the arrow.

ZING! The arrow zipped around and between the doctor's legs. It flew like a hawk. The doctor tripped and fell.

"Wow! Did you see that arrow, Zack?" Kerry asked.

"That's her Falcon Eye arrow," Zack said. "It can fly in any direction. It can even fly in circles."

Kerry's mom brought snacks into the living room. "Are you two watching Brave Bowie again?" she asked.

"Of course!" Kerry said. "We're learning how to become superheroes."

"It doesn't look too tough," Zack said.
"All we need are cool bows and arrows.
We'll be saving the city from danger in
no time."

Kerry's mom grinned. "Zack, your parents and I know how much you and Kerry love Brave Bowie," she said. "So, we have an idea. Would you two like to take archery lessons?"

Kerry and Zack looked at each other and smiled. Their eyes got big. "YES!" they shouted together.

"OK!" Kerry's mom said. "I'll take you both to the archery range tomorrow morning. There you'll learn how to become archers."

Kerry and Zack cheered. "We're going to be superheroes!" they said.

Chapter 2
NOT SO EASY

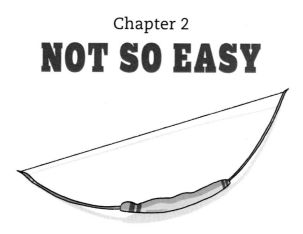

The next day, Kerry's mom took Kerry and Zack to Archers' Club. It was an indoor archery range. A teacher named Tia checked in the kids.

"You two ready for an archery lesson today?" Tia asked.

"Yes!" Kerry said. "My friend Zack and I love Brave Bowie. We're going to be superheroes like her."

Tia smiled. "Follow me," she said. "The place where you're going to shoot is called your station."

Kerry and Zack followed Tia. Outside their station were two bows and some arrows. The friends each picked up a bow and an arrow. Then they aimed.

"Wait, wait, wait!" Tia said. "Never load and aim your arrows outside your station. That's not safe. You have to be *inside*. You could hurt someone if you shoot in an open area."

Kerry and Zack took the arrows off their bows. "Sorry," they said.

"That's okay," Tia said. "I know you're excited." She put a leather strap on Kerry's arm. Zack got one too. The straps would keep their arms safe from the bowstring and arrow while shooting.

Tia showed Kerry and Zack how to shoot from their station.

"Now, the hand you hold the bow with is your bow hand," Tia said. "You pull back the bowstring with your other hand. Plant your feet, load your arrow, and aim at the target. Then let go."

Kerry tried first. She pulled back on
the bowstring. She aimed and let go. Her
arrow landed a few feet short of the target.

Zack went next. His arrow barely made it halfway.

"I don't think that was a Falcon Eye arrow," Zack said jokingly.

"This is harder than I thought it would be," Kerry said.

Chapter 3
A NEW TARGET

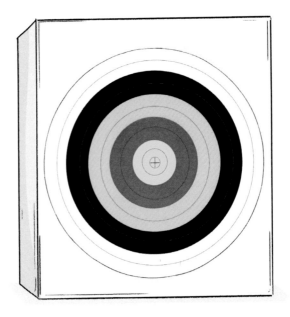

Neither Kerry nor Zack could hit the target.

"We'll never be superheroes if we can't hit the target," Zack said.

Kerry and Zack looked over at the station next to theirs. A teenage girl was shooting. She made one bull's-eye, then another, and another!

"She's awesome!" Kerry said.

"Did you see those bull's-eyes?" Zack asked.

Tia grinned and called to the girl. "Aliyah, come meet my new students," she said.

The girl hurried over. Kerry and Zack stood quietly. They didn't know what to say. Then Zack asked, "Are you Brave Bowie?"

"No," the girl laughed. "My name's Aliyah. I'm on the archery team. I've been practicing for years."

Kerry smiled. "I'm Kerry, and this is Zack," she said. "This is our first day here. We can't even hit the target."

"It takes practice to become a good archer," Aliyah said. "My first time, I hit everything *except* the target!"

"Really?" Kerry said.

"The more I practiced, the better I got," Aliyah said. "Let's see you two try shooting again."

Kerry went first. She loaded her arrow and aimed. She let go. *THWIP!* Her arrow hit the target. "I did it!" she cried. "It's not a bull's-eye, but I hit the target!"

Then Zack tried. *THWIP!* "I hit the target too!" he said.

Kerry and Zack kept practicing until Kerry's mom picked them up.

"Can we come back tomorrow?" Kerry asked her mom. "Zack and I need more practice. We want to be on the archery team, like Aliyah."

"I thought you two wanted to be superheroes," Kerry's mom said.

"Not anymore," Kerry said. "We're aiming higher. Being a real archer is way cooler!"

CAN YOU HIT IT?

Have fun while building your aiming skills with this tabletop game.

What You Need:
- at least one friend
- 10 clean, empty tin cans
- markers
- rubber bands
- a timer

What You Do:
1. Draw a bull's-eye on the side of each can.
2. On a table, stack the cans in a pyramid.
3. Set the timer for 30 seconds. Use your fingers to shoot rubber bands at the bull's-eyes until time's up. Be sure to sit at least three arm-lengths away from the cans.
4. Score 1 point for every target you hit on the bottom row, 5 points for the next row, 10 points for the next, and 20 points for the top can. The person with the highest total wins!

REPLAY IT

Take another look at this illustration. Have you ever struggled with a new sport or activity? How do you think Zack is feeling at this moment? Pretend you are Zack and write a letter to your grandparents about it.

ABOUT THE AUTHOR

Shawn Pryor is the creator and co-author of the graphic novel mystery series Cash & Carrie, co-creator and author of the 2019 GLYPH-nominated football/drama series Force, and author of *Kentucky Kaiju* and *Jake Maddox: Diamond Double Play*. In his free time, he enjoys reading, cooking, listening to streaming music playlists, and talking about why Zack from the Mighty Morphin Power Rangers is the greatest superhero of all time.

ABOUT THE ILLUSTRATOR

Diego Funck designs and illustrates children's books and other publications, often working with a Belgian illustration team called Coco Zool. Since 2005, his work has appeared in gallery shows in Belgium, France, and England. When he's not drawing or painting, Diego loves to watch movie trailers and dig in his vegetable garden. He currently lives in Brussels, Belgium.